Weird
School Day

There are lots of Early Reader stories you might enjoy.

Look at the back of the book or, for a complete list, visit www.orionbooks.co.uk

Weird School Day

By Alan, Rachel
and Megan Gibbons

Illustrated by
Jane Porter

Orion
Children's Books

First published in Great Britain in 2015
by Orion Children's Books
a division of the Orion Publishing Group Ltd
Orion House
5 Upper Saint Martin's Lane
London WC2H 9EA
An Hachette UK Company

1 3 5 7 9 10 8 6 4 2

Text © Alan Gibbons, Rachel Gibbons and Megan Gibbons 2015
Illustrations © Jane Porter 2015

The moral right of Alan Gibbons, Rachel Gibbons and
Megan Gibbons and Jane Porter to be identified as authors
and illustrator of this work has been asserted.

The Orion Publishing Group's policy is to use papers that are natural,
renewable and recyclable products and made from wood grown in
sustainable forests. The logging and manufacturing processes are expected
to conform to the environmental regulations of the country of origin.

ISBN 978 1 4440 1278 1

A catalogue record for this book
is available from the British Library.

Printed and bound in China

www.orionbooks.co.uk

To all at Ykids, Bootle.

Contents

One

Nobody knew how it started.
Nobody knew what made it
happen. It just did.

One day the animals were the way they had always been.

Then everything went weird.

The moment Katie Cat opened her eyes she knew something was wrong. She felt very odd.

She sat up in bed and yawned.
But she didn't say **miaow**.
She said **too-wit-too-woo**!

"That's funny," she thought.
"No, that's … *weird*!"

The **too-wit-too-woo** wasn't all. When she tried to lick her grey fur she found her mouth was full of ...

... feathers.

She spat and spluttered.
"Mum!" she wailed.
But it came out
too-wit-too-wum.

Two

Katie ran into the bathroom and
saw herself in the mirror.

She couldn't believe her eyes. She was half-cat ... half-owl!

Katie was so surprised that she jumped and hit her head on the ceiling.

"How did this happen?"
she said to herself.

"I've got

feathers

and fur

and whiskers

and wings.

I'm all mixed up."

Then she remembered something important.
"It's my first day at school,"
she moaned. "I've been looking
forward to it all summer.
This is terrible."

Mum came up the stairs.
"Is something wrong?" she asked.

"No, Mum," Katie said.
"I was playing a game."

What am I going to do,
she thought.

She tried to put her uniform on.

Her wings kept popping out.

She knocked a book off her table.

Bang.

She knocked a picture off the wall.

Crash.

"What are you doing?" Mum called.
"Nothing," Katie said. "I'm just getting ready."

Three

Oh dear, oh dear, oh dear, she thought. I can't be late on my first day. What *am* I going to do?

She crept downstairs and shot out
of the door.

She wasn't going to stop for anything. She tucked her wings in tight and kept her head low. Nobody can see me like this, she thought.

By the time she got to school, everyone was going in. She did her best to hide her face.

When she got into class, she
looked up and gasped with
surprise.

Four

She wasn't the only one who was all mixed up. Katie saw her best friend, Penny Pig.

Penny wasn't just a pig any more. Instead of her curly, pink tail, she now had a big, bushy grey tail. It was nearly as big as she was!

"Penny," Katie said. "You're not a pig or a squirrel. You're a **Piggel**."

"That's nothing," Penny said,
"you're part cat, part owl ...
you're a ... Miaowl."

They stared at each other.

Then they burst out laughing.

"You look  ,"

Katie said.

"You look **funny** ,"

Penny said.

"You look **strange** ,"

Katie chuckled.

That's when something big flew
through the window.

It was Tony Pony. Tony wasn't just a pony any more.

He had a pair of huge, golden wings.

"Whee!" he neighed.
He was a **Poneagle**.

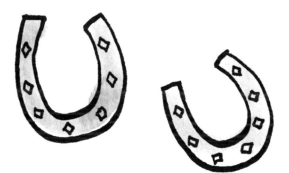

Five

Katie looked around and saw
the weirdest animal yet. It was
Ricky Rabbit.

He had strong hind legs like a
rabbit and a pair of claws like
a crab. He also had a shell.

He hopped the way a rabbit does, but there was something different about him.

"Look," Penny said, "he's hopping *side*ways!"

She was right. Ricky hopped
into the wall and bounced off.
He looked very puzzled.

"He's a **Crabbit**," Katie said. "This is getting weirder by the minute."

Moments later somebody wailed loudly. It was Dabby Dog.

"I popped my birthday balloon," he cried.

Katie and Penny stared at him.
He wasn't just a puppy anymore.
There was one big difference.
His back was covered in pointy
spikes.

"He's a hedgehound!" Penny exclaimed. "What is going on around here?"

Six

That's when the door started to
open. The animals stopped talking.

"I'm Mrs Creature," said a voice.
"I'm your teacher. What's this
racket?"
"We're all mixed up!" Katie said.
"What do we do?"

"Yes, what do we do?" said
Penny Pig, Tony Pony, Ricky
Rabbit and Dabby Dog.

Mrs Creature walked into the
room. The animals stared.

She had fangs and fur, but she
had hooves too. She was
half-wolf, half-donkey.

"So you're …"

"Yes, I'm a **Wonkey**. Something very strange is going on here.

Maybe tomorrow everything
will be back to normal."

Only it wasn't. In fact, the world
of the Weirdibeasts was about
to get weirder still. But that's
another story!

What are you going to read next?

Have more adventures with Horrid Henry,

or save the day with Anthony Ant!

Become a superhero with Monstar,

float off to sea with Algy,

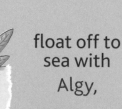

or have your very own **Pirates' Picnic.**

Grow carrots with

Lottie and Dottie,

make magic with The Witch Dog,

and cast a spell with

The Three Little Magicians.

Enjoy all the Early Readers.